ME + MATH = HEADACHE

Me + you = Friendship

Lee Wardlaw

Story by Lee Wardlaw
Illustrated by Deborah Stouffer

For Hope, Keo, Lisa, Marni and Susie—
with thanks for easing the headaches of writing—L.W.

To my mother for her generous gift of time and love,
and to Baby Loren, my newest inspiration—D.S.

LIBRARY OF CONGRESS CATALOGING-IN-PUBLICATION DATA

Wardlaw, Lee, 1955–
    Me + math = headache.

    Summary: Third grader Jeffrey hates math and is sure an assignment
to find three uses for math outside of school is ridiculous.
[1. Mathematics—Fiction]   I. Deborah Stouffer, 1950, ill.
II. Title.   III. Title: Me and math equals headache.
IV. Title: Me plus math equals headache.
P27.W2174Me   1986   [Fic]   86-20305
ISBN 0-931093-07-4
Second printing, 1989

RED HEN PRESS
P.O. Box 419
Summerland, CA 93067

CHAPTER ONE

I flunked another math test today.

I thought the older I got, the smarter I'd get too. Guess I thought wrong. Third grade math is even harder than second grade math.

At the top of my paper Miss Simmons wrote a big red "F" and a note that says "See me after school." I hate it when Miss Simmons uses a red pencil.

Richard Jensen, who sits next to me, got "B+"on his math test. I know because I peeked at his paper when Miss Simmons put it on his desk.

When Richard tried to look at my paper, I covered it with my hands. I don't like Richard Jensen. He has sneaky eyes.

My best friends, Craig Zeisloft and Teresa Mendoza, got "Bs" on their tests, too. When they saw my paper, Craig gave a long, low whistle. Teresa chomped her gum in a real thoughtful way and said, "Wow, Jeffrey. *Another* 'F'?"

Richard overheard her. "Hey, you must be pretty dumb, Jeffrey," he said.

"I am not!" I punched Richard in the arm when Miss Simmons wasn't looking. "And who cares, anyway? I hate math!"

After school, Miss Simmons asked me why I thought I flunked the math test. I told her our rhinoceros got loose on 23rd Street and we had to look for him. I told her it took all night and I didn't have time to study.

Miss Simmon's left eye winked funny. Her left eye always does that when she thinks we've told a lie. I wasn't really lying. Our rhinoceros could've gotten loose. If we had one.

"Jeffrey," Miss Simmons said, "you're one of my brightest students. But you seem to have a very

hard time with math. What do you think the problem is?"

I didn't say anything. I just looked down at my shoes. They're white with green racing stripes to help me run very fast.

"Jeffrey, look at me."

I looked up. How could anyone as pretty as Miss Simmons teach something as awful as math?

"Jeffrey, maybe I can help you if you tell me how you feel about math."

I thought hard about my answer. If I told Miss Simmons I loved math, she'd know I was lying. But if I told her I hated math, maybe she'd kick me out of school. Wow! That'd be great! Maybe I could go to Africa and hunt rhinoceros. Mom wouldn't like that too much, but I had to take a chance.

"I hate math," I said. "I just hate it. It's dumb. Everytime I look at all those stupid numbers I get a headache."

Miss Simmons played with a pencil on her desk.

"Why do you think we need all those stupid numbers, Jeffrey?"

"We don't--that's what's so dumb," I said. "Once I get out of school, I'll never use math again. Never!" I took a deep breath. "I'm tired of math, Miss Simmons. I don't want to study it anymore."

There. I'd said it. I waited for Miss Simmons to shout, "Jeffrey--leave school at once!" But instead, she smiled!

"I'm glad you were honest with me, Jeffrey. And I understand exactly how you feel."

"You *do* ?"

"Of course. I wouldn't want to learn a subject either if I thought it was dumb." Miss Simmons wrote something on a piece of paper. Then she folded the paper and handed it to me. "Here. This is a special homework assignment for you. Maybe it will help you to understand just how important math is."

I gulped. "You mean, it's math homework?"

"Yes, it is."

Rats! My head started to hurt just thinking about it. Suddenly, I felt desperate. "Miss Simmons, aren't you going to kick me out of school?"

She laughed. "No, Jeffrey. I think I'd like to have you in my class a little longer. We need to work together to clear up this math problem of yours." Miss Simmons started to erase the chalkboard. "By the way, did you ever find your rhinoceros?"

"Uh--yeah. He was hiding in the elevator."

"Oh." Miss Simmons went back to her chalkboard. "Well, I'm sure you're anxious to get home, Jeffrey. See you tomorrow."

I got my jacket from the closet and walked slowly outside. Then I remembered my homework. What kind of special assignment could it be? I unfolded the paper. This is what it said:

FIND THREE IMPORTANT THINGS YOU NEED MATH FOR BESIDES A CLASS IN SCHOOL.

Oh, no! I stuffed the paper in my pocket. Miss Simmons was the worst teacher I'd ever had. And I used to think she was pretty. I got so mad, I stomped out of the school yard thinking, I-hate-math. I-hate-math. I-hate-math.

CHAPTER TWO

"Hi, Jeffrey," Craig said. "Ready to go?"

He and Teresa were waiting for me at the school gate. Since we all live in the same apartment building, we walk home together every day. Mom doesn't like me walking home alone. Afraid I'll get hit by a car or something. She never worries when I'm with Craig, though. He's the tallest kid in our class and has bright red hair. He'd make a good stop sign.

"Jeffrey, ready to go?" Craig repeated.

I stomped past him without a word. I felt too mad at Miss Simmons to be nice to anyone, even my best friends.

Craig and Teresa followed me down the street. I

could hear Teresa chomping her bubble gum. Grape today, so it must be Tuesday. Teresa chews a different flavor every day. Banana on Monday, strawberry on Wednesday, root beer on Thursday, regular on Friday, cinnamon on Saturday. On Sundays, she chews all the flavors at once. Gross!

"Hey, what did Miss Simmons want?" Teresa asked. "Are you going to flunk out of school? Do you have to get a math tutor?"

I didn't say anything.

"My brother had a math tutor once," Craig said. "She was real old and ugly and picked her nose when she thought no one was looking. She gave my brother about a million little cards with math problems on them. Like two-plus-three on one side, and the answer on the back. He had to take them on vacation and pratice and practice until he had them memorized. Took him all summer. He was pretty dumb."

"Will you have to take those cards home during Christmas vacation?" Teresa asked me.

I turned and glared at her. She blew a bubble the size of a tennis ball. Then she chomped it like it was a tennis ball.

"Well? Will you?" she asked.

I was getting madder by the minute. I kicked a stone out of my way and kept on stomping.

"I guess you *are* dumb," Teresa said. Chomp, chomp. POP.

"I--AM--NOT--DUMB!" I shouted.

Craig and Teresa put their arms around each other and sang, "Jeff got an F! Jeff is a bo-zo! He'll have to get a tutor, who picks her no-zo!"

I whirled around. "Shut up!" I yelled. "You aren't my friends anymore!" I was breathing very hard. I glared at Teresa. "I hope a big bubble gets stuck in your hair and your mother has to cut it all off! And you--" I pointed at Craig. "I hope you get so tall, they have to put you in a zoo--with the giraffes!"

Craig looked very surprised. I thought Teresa might cry. But who cared? I turned around and ran

six blocks before I looked back. They weren't following me. Good. Today I hated Craig and Teresa, even more than math. And that's a lot of hate.

CHAPTER THREE

I was in a door-slamming mood. But I couldn't go home to do that. Dad's a writer and likes the house quiet in the afternoons. Says he can think better that way. I can't think at all when I'm trying to do math, no matter how quiet it is.

I didn't want to go home anyway. Juliet would be there by now. Juliet's my sister. My older sister. She thinks she's wonderful just because she's thirteen and gets to paint her fingernails. Big deal. Juliet yells at me a lot in a high screechy voice that sounds like a parakeet I had once that died.

I finally decided to visit my mom. I kind of felt like talking, and Mom's a good listener. She understands a lot of things, too.

I hurried to the supermarket. Mom's a checker. She runs this neat cash register. It's a new computer kind that beeps. I think being a checker would be fun, but I'd get hungry looking at doughnuts and hot dogs and frozen pizzas all day long.

At the supermarket, I walked straight to the third lane where Mom works. I was about to say hello when a lady with pink hair pushed me out of the way with her purse.

"Oh, no you don't, kid," she said. "I was here first. Just wait your turn."

"She's my mom," I said, pointing. "I just wanted to say hello."

"I don't care if she's your uncle. I was here first and you'll have to wait till I'm finished. Children today have no manners." The lady with pink hair pushed her food toward Mom. "Here's everything I need. Hurry. I'm late."

Mom gave me one of her Hello-Jeffrey-it's-nice-to-see- you-please-be-patient smiles. I smiled back, then stared at the lady with pink hair. She was buying enough dog food to feed a rhinoceros for a year! I don't think rhinoceroses like dog food, though. Maybe peanut butter.

BEEP! Mom looked up from the cash register. "Anything else, ma'am? All right, that will be cleven dollars and fifty-two cents."

The lady with pink hair opened her purse, then scowled at me as if I was a burglar in disguise. Quickly she pulled out her money, counted it and handed it to Mom.

"I'm sorry, ma'am," Mom said. "There are only ten dollars here. I need one more dollar and fifty-two cents, please."

"I don't know what you mean," the lady said. Her face was turning the same color as her hair. "I gave you the exact amount."

Mom shook her head. "I'm sorry, ma'am. See? There's only ten dollars here."

"Well--I've had enough of *this* store!" The lady with pink hair grabbed her money and almost crashed into a shopping cart as she ran out the door.

She didn't take any of her dog food. I hoped her dog wasn't too hungry.

"What's wrong with her?" I asked Mom.

"She's embarrassed, Jeffrey." Mom shook her head. "Some people just aren't very good at making change."

My head started to hurt. "You mean you need math to buy dog food?" I asked.

Mom laughed. "Of course. You know that. Remember last Christmas when you divided your allowance money for presents?"

I nodded. I'd spent five dollars on both Mom and Dad--but only seventy-five cents on Juliet. That's all she deserved.

"Well, without simple math, like adding and subtracting," Mom continued, "you'd never have been able to figure out how much money to spend on us. It's the same with everything you buy."

I scowled down at my shoes.

"Jeffrey?"

I glanced up. Mom leaned over the counter and felt my forehead with the back of her hand. "Do you feel all right, Jeffrey? You look a little flushed."

"Yeah. I'm okay." I couldn't tell Mom about my headache now. She just wouldn't understand.

A couple of people with loaded food carts lined up at Mom's checkstand.

"Back to work!" she said, smiling. "Be careful going home, Jeffrey. You're alone today, aren't you? Where are Craig and Teresa? See you at dinner."

Outside I leaned against the building, then took my homework assignment from my pocket. I used my knee as a desk and wrote:

THREE IMPORTANT THINGS YOU NEED MATH FOR. NUMBER ONE. YOU NEED MATH TO COUNT MONEY SO YOU CAN BUY DOG FOOD AND OTHER STUFF.

I stared at the paper for awhile, then shoved it back into my pocket. I figured when I got older I'd hire a butler to buy things for me. That way, I'd never have to use math again.

CHAPTER FOUR

Mmmmmm. Peanut butter cookies! I could smell them the minute I walked into our apartment.

I forgot all about my headache and hurried into the kitchen. Juliet was peering into the oven. Dad stood at the counter, holding a chapter from his new book in one hand and a mixing spoon in the other.

Juliet ignored me, but Dad said, "Hi Jeffrey!"

"You're baking?" I couldn't hide the surprise in my voice. Dad's not the greatest cook. He even has problems opening a box of corn flakes.

Dad didn't say anything. He just stared at me.

Juliet took a pan of cookies out of the oven. They smelled so good! I reached for a hot one.

"Hey!" Juliet yelled. "Leave those cookies alone. Daaa-aaad, Jeffrey's trying to eat a cookie!"

"Come on, Juliet," I said. "You don't *own* those cookies."

"I don't see why Jeffrey can't have one, Juliet," Dad said. He put his chapter down and washed his hands in the sink. "Your brother looks as if he had a hard day at school." Dad smiled. "Go ahead, Jeffrey. Take one. You can be our official taster."

My mouth watered just looking at all those cookies cooling on the counter. The peanut smell tickled my nose. I snatched at the biggest cookie and stuffed it in my mouth.

"Well?" Dad asked. "How are they?"

"Yeah," Juliet said. She leaned against the counter, arms folded across her chest, looking very pleased with herself. I kind of wanted to say the cookies were awful, just so she'd stop looking so smug. Except--the cookies *were* awful!

"Would you like a glass of milk?" Dad wasn't smiling anymore. "What's the matter, Jeffrey? Are you sick?"

I handed him a cookie. "Here, Dad--you taste one." I didn't want to hurt his feelings.

Dad bit into the cookie. Then he kind of coughed and swallowed real fast. "They are a bit-- well, um, different."

"Too much salt," I explained. "Are you sure you measured everything right?"

"Of course we did," Juliet said in disgust.

"Well, I think we did," Dad said.

"Oh-oh." Juliet sneaked out of the kitchen.

"Where's that recipe card?" Dad asked. He found it under a mound of spilled flour. "Now, it says here . . . Oh." He cleared his throat. "Well, anyone could've made this mistake. See, I was working on that chapter--had a few problems with paragraph two--and I guess I wasn't . . . well, I must not've been paying close attention."

Poor Dad. I shook my head and left him in the

kitchen, staring sadly at all those cookies. It was part Juliet's fault. She should've double-checked the recipe. I help Mom bake cookies all the time. She says we always need to measure everything carefully. And I always do, even though I hate it. Measuring reminds me too much of . . .

Oh, no. Math again!

I scuffed slowly into my bedroom and sat down at my desk. Then I took out my homework. On the paper I wrote:

NUMBER TWO. YOU NEED MATH TO MEASURE STUFF FOR BAKING PEANUT BUTTER COOKIES OR ELSE THEY TASTE *AWFUL*.

I stared at the paper a long time. Now I knew two important things I needed math for. Buying food and baking cookies. But I wouldn't ever need math for anything else.

Or would I?

CHAPTER FIVE

I stayed in my room most of the afternoon. Craig Zeisloft called me on the phone four times, but I told Dad I had lots of homework and couldn't talk. I didn't really have homework--except for the math assignment. But I didn't feel like talking to Craig after the way he and Teresa had laughed at me. I wondered if I'd ever talk to those two again. Best friends, HA!

Everytime I looked at my math assignment my headache got worse. Finally I just turned the paper over the started to doodle.

ME + MATH = HEADACHE

ME x MATH = I HATE MATH

ME ÷ MATH = LOTS OF MEs HATING MATH

Then I thought of a great one.

ME − MATH = 🙂

After that, I drew a big purple rhinoceros standing on top of the word math. I made him look like he was smashing the word real thin. By the time I finished coloring the rhinoceros, Mom was home.

"Jeffery!" she called. "Time for dinner!"

Macaroni and cheese and pork chops. Usually I can eat a whole bathtub full of pork chops. But not that night. My stomach felt tight, like a fist. I was too mad to eat. I was mad at Craig and Teresa and Miss Simmons. I even felt mad at those stupid peanut butter cookies.

"Did you have a good day at school, Jeffrey?" Mom asked.

"It was okay." I poured almost the whole bottle of Italian dressing on my salad and watched the lettuce float around.

"Moooo-ooom!" Juliet screeched. "Jeffrey used all the salad dressing!"

I made a face at Juliet. "Yeah? Well, you sound like a rhinoceros!"

"Daaaa--aaad! Jeffrey called me, a rhinoceros!"

"Jeffrey, that was rude." Dad had a stern look on his face. "Apologize to your sister."

"I'm sorry," I mumbled. But I wasn't saying it to her. I was apologizing to all the rhinoceroses in the world.

"You haven't been acting like yourself today, Jeffrey," Mom said. "Did something bad happen at school? Do you want to talk about it?"

Mom sounded so nice I almost wanted to cry. Maybe she *would* understand. I stirred the lettuce in my salad bowl and drowned a piece of carrot with my fork. Finally I said, "I flunked another math test today."

Juliet giggled. "You are so dumb. I never flunked a math test in my whole life."

"That's true," Dad said. He pointed his fork at her. "But I seem to remember a lot of 'Fs' on your spelling tests."

Juliet stopped laughing. I made another face at her. She looked away, drinking her milk.

"Flunking a test isn't anything to be ashamed about," Mom said. "And it doesn't mean you're dumb. It just means you have to study a little harder than other people. Or maybe get extra help from a friend. Juliet is better in math than you are. But you're better in spelling. Everyone has something they do well, and something they don't do very well." Mom smiled. "Dad and I will be glad to help you with your math, Jeffrey. And if that's not enough, we can make arrangements to get you a tutor."

Suddenly, I pictured a lady with pink hair, picking her nose and shoving millions of numbers in my face. My head pounded. I leaped out of my chair. "I'm not getting a tutor!" I yelled. "I'm not dumb and I don't need help with math. I hate math! It's stupid and it gives me a headache and I want to go someplace where I won't ever have to use it again. And--and I'm not hungry!"

I ran to my room and slammed the door.

CHAPTER SIX

I flopped down on my bed and stared up at the ceiling. I hadn't meant to yell at Mom and Dad like that. What would happen next? Would Dad spank me? I probably wouldn't be allowed to watch television for a month.

I could hear voices in the kitchen. Every now and then someone said my name. I hate it when people talk about me and I'm not there.

After awhile, there was a knock on my door.

"Go away," I said. My voice was very cool.

"Jeffrey," Dad said, "I know you're upset, but you have a couple of visitors. May I send them in?"

Who could be here to see me? I wondered. "Well--okay."

The door opened. In walked Craig and Teresa!

"What do *you* want?" I asked, still looking at the ceiling.

"We came to apologize," Teresa said. "We're sorry we said you were dumb. You're not dumb, Jeffrey. You're our friend."

"Yeah," Craig said.

I didn't say anything. I wasn't sure I could forgive them.

"You made me feel awful," I said.

"We were only teasing," Craig explained. "But I guess it wasn't very funny. We're really sorry."

The room was quiet. I couldn't even hear Teresa chewing her gum. Should I forgive them? Hating math was bad enough. I decided I didn't need to hate my friends, too.

"Well--okay," I said.

Craig grinned at me. Teresa smiled, too. She popped a huge grape bubble. I didn't mind this time. It was a happy sound, like balloons popping at a birthday party.

"What did Miss Simmons say this afternoon?"

Craig asked. He and Teresa sat down on the floor.

I showed them my homework assignment. "I'm supposed to find three important things I need math for. I have two answers, but I can't think of a third." I punched my pillow. "I hate math so much. I don't want to finish this assignment. I want to go some place where no one ever uses math. Like Africa."

"So, go to Africa," Craig said.

I thought for a minute. "Sure, why not? I don't need to stay here. I can go to Africa and hunt rhinoceroses." I shut my eyes. Suddenly I could picture myself with my foot on the chest of the biggest rhinoceros in the world. Of course, I'd caught him single-handed and had won a big gold trophy. Rhinoceros burgers for everyone!

Teresa's voice interrupted my daydream. "Can I go to Africa with you? I don't like math much, either."

"Well, if Teresa's going, so am I," Craig said.

"Okay." I jumped off the bed. "Let's go right away."

"I don't know," Craig said, shaking his head. "I have a dentist appointment tomorrow."

"They have dentists in Africa, don't they?" Teresa asked.

"I guess so." Craig didn't look too sure.

"Great," I said. "It's all settled. Teresa, run home and get some food. Craig, you're in charge of blankets. I'll find a flashlight and a map. We'll meet in the lobby in fifteen minutes. Okay?"

Craig and Teresa nodded.

"And don't let anyone see you," I added. "If we're caught, we could get in trouble."

My friends left the room quietly. I waited a few minutes till I was sure they were gone. I opened my door a crack and peeked into the hall. Mom and Dad's voices came from the kitchen. Good. I was safe.

Very quietly, I crept into my parents' bedroom and took the flashlight Mom keeps beside her bed in case of burglars. Then I tiptoed into Dad's office.

I couldn't find a map, so I grabbed the world atlas instead.

"What are you doing in here? You know you're not supposed to be in here without Dad's permission!"

My heart froze. I whirled around. Juliet!

"And what are you doing with Dad's atlas?" she demanded. "Put it back or I'm telling."

"Go ahead," I said. "I don't care. I won't be living here anymore, anyway."

"Oh, yeah?" Juliet had her hands on her hips. "And just where do you think you're going?"

"Africa!" I scooped up the atlas and ran past Juliet as fast as I could. I was halfway to the elevator when I heard her yell.

"Daaaa-aaad! Jeffrey says he's going to AFRICA!"

CHAPTER SEVEN

Craig and Teresa were waiting for me in the lobby.

"Did anyone see you leave?" I asked.

Craig shook his head.

"Mom saw me taking the food," Teresa said. "I told her we were having a picnic in the elevator." She giggled. "All Mom said was, 'Oh--have a nice time, dear.' "

"What did you bring to eat?" I asked. My stomach was growling. I wished I'd eaten those pork chops.

Teresa poked her nose into a large grocery bag. "Pickles, meat loaf, diet Kool-aid, crackers and six flavors of bubble gum."

UGH. My stomach did a double flip. But I couldn't complain. It was nice of Teresa to bring the food.

"Are we ready?" I asked.

Craig held up three blankets.

"Okay, then. Let's go!"

The street wasn't very dark, but I turned on the flashlight, anyway. The beam made the sidewalk sparkle. I wondered what sort of exciting things would happen on our trip.

"I'm tired," Teresa said after awhile. "How far have we walked?"

"I'm not sure," I answered. "We passed the school about ten minutes ago."

"Let's rest." Craig sat down on the curb. "Did you bring the map, Jeffrey? Look up Africa and see how far we have to go."

I opened the atlas under the glow of a street lamp. "This says Africa is over 3,000 miles away."

Craig did his low whistle. "That's a long walk."

"Yeah," Teresa agreed. "We might run out of gum. How long will it take to walk that far?"

"I'll figure it out." I took a pencil and paper from my pocket. "How many miles can you walk a day?" I asked Teresa.

She chomped her gum for a few seconds. "Oh, I guess about ten."

"How about you, Craig?"

"The same. Ten miles a day."

I scribbled down the numbers. "Well, if Africa is 3,000 miles away, and we can walk ten miles a day, the problem looks like this:

$$10 \overline{)3,000}$$

"3,000 divided by ten is three hundred. So it'll take us three hundred days to get to Africa."

Suddenly, a strange feeling came over me.

"Hey," I said. "I just did a math problem and my head doesn't hurt a bit. In fact, I feel pretty good!"

Craig looked sad. "I guess we'd even have to do math in Africa."

I nodded. "Guess you're right." I pulled my jacket tighter around me. "Brrrrr, it's getting cold."

"Yeah," Craig said. He put one of the blankets around his shoulders. "Maybe we should head home."

"What'll we do with all this food?" I asked.

"Let's have a picnic in the elevator," Teresa suggested.

Craig smiled. "Good idea. Besides, we couldn't have walked to Africa anyway."

"Why not?" Teresa asked.

"I've been looking at this map. Africa is across the Atlantic Ocean. We'd have to *swim* there!"

"That's right--I forgot," I said. "And I can't swim!"

Teresa laughed. "Neither can I. And the meat loaf would've gotten soggy."

We all laughed then, and practically ran the whole way home. I was never so glad to see our apartment building. It felt good to see the elevator, too. It was warm inside, especially with my two best friends sitting beside me.

After we'd eaten all of Teresa's meat loaf and pickles, I decided we'd better go home. It was getting late and I was worried that Mom and Dad would be mad at me. But when I hurried into the apartment, Mom just gave me a big hug and a kiss and said, "Time for bed."

I put on my pajamas and brushed my teeth. My bed looked warm and comfortable, but I didn't crawl into it right away. I had something important to do first.

I took out my homework assignment. On the paper I wrote:

NUMBER THREE. YOU NEED MATH TO FIGURE OUT HOW FAR IT IS TO AFRICA AND HOW LONG IT WOULD TAKE TO WALK (OR SWIM) THERE.

Now I was ready for bed. I snuggled deep into my blankets. I felt so tired. I hoped I wouldn't dream about noisy rhinoceroses.

CHAPTER EIGHT

The next morning I folded my homework as carefully as I could and put it in my pocket. A cinnamony smell drifted into my room. French toast for breakfast! I hoped Dad wasn't cooking.

"You must feel better this morning," Mom said, after I'd eaten five pieces of toast. (Mom had cooked.)

"I do. A little." I drank my milk. "Hey, Mom, if we decide to get a math tutor, would I have to see her *every* day? And if I didn't like her--I mean, if she had a disgusting habit or something--could I get somebody else?"

Mom smiled. "Those are two very important questions," she said. "How about if you, Dad and I discuss it tonight, after dinner?"

"Sure." I grabbed my lunch sack. I was ready to run out the door when Dad came into the kitchen. He sipped his coffee, looking thoughtful.

"What should I do with all these cookies?" he asked. They were still on the counter.

"Give them to Mrs. Hanson's dog," Juliet said. "He barks too loud, anyway."

Mom gave Juliet a stern look. "Throw them out," she said to Dad.

He sighed. "Guess I might as well."

"Don't feel bad," I said to him. "It's nothing to feel ashamed about. Baking cookies is just something you're not very good at. Like me and math."

Dad chuckled. "I know, I know."

Suddenly, I had an idea. It was a great way to get back at Richard Jensen for laughing at me.

"Hey, Dad, I'll throw these out for you on my way to school."

"All right."

I got a paper sack from the cupboard, then

glanced around to make sure no one was watching me. Dad was helping Mom wash the dishes. Juliet was still eating her breakfast. Good. I scooped the cookies into the sack.

"Goodbye!" I called. "I'm going to school."

I met Teresa and Craig in the elevator. "What's in the sack?" they asked.

"You'll find out later," I said.

At school I walked right up to Miss Simmons. "Here's my homework," I announced. This time I looked her in the eye.

Miss Simmons read my paper. "This is good, Jeffrey," she said with a smile. "I can tell you put a lot of thought into it. How do you feel about math now?"

I thought hard about my answer. If I told Miss Simmons I loved math, she'd know I was lying. But for some reason, I wasn't sure I hated math anymore.

"I don't like math very much," I said. "It's hard for me, but--," I took a deep breath. "But I guess

it's an important thing to learn."

"Yes, it is," Miss Simmons said. "But I'll let you in on a little secret." She lowered her voice to a whisper. "I don't like math very much, either."

We smiled at each other. Then Miss Simmons said, "You must feel very proud, Jeffrey. A fine job on your homework. Not many students realize how important math is. I wish there were some way you could help convince them."

"I have the perfect way," I said with a grin. I held up the sack I'd brought from home. Then in a loud voice, I said to the class, "Would anybody like a peanut butter cookie?"

The End